Nº1 CAR
SPOTTER

and the Broken Road

by Atinuke

illustrated by Warwick Johnson Cadwell

WALKER
BOOKS

First published in Great Britain 2015 by Walker Books Ltd
87 Vauxhall Walk, London SE11 5HJ

2 4 6 8 10 9 7 5 3 1

Text © 2015 by Atinuke
Illustrations © 2015 Warwick Johnson Cadwell

The right of Atinuke and Warwick Johnson Cadwell to be identified as
author and illustrator respectively of this work has been asserted by them
in accordance with the Copyright, Designs and Patents Act 1988

This book has been typeset in Stempel Schneidler and WJCadwell

Printed and bound in Great Britain by Clays Ltd, St Ives plc

British Library Cataloguing in Publication Data:
a catalogue record for this book is
available from the British Library

ISBN 978-1-4063-4346-5

www.walker.co.uk

For Tiger,
who got this book written
A.

To my gang as ever,
D, S, H and W
W. JC.

The Broken Road

I am the No. 1 car spotter. The No. 1 car spotter in my village. The No. 1 car spotter in my country. I might even be the No. 1 car spotter on the whole entire continent of Africa. It is entirely possible.

A No. 1 road runs past my village. And many fine-fine cars drive along this road, passing our village on their way from one city to another.

If you are lucky those cars will stop in front of Mama Coca-Cola's No. 1 chop-house restaurant. That is where my sister, Sissy, likes to spot cars.

Dawoo! Audi! Toyota!

My tight friend, Coca-Cola, and my cousins, Emergency and Tuesday, are quicker than Sissy. They can spot a car as it drives past the village.

Peugeot! Honda! Volvo!

But I am the No. 1 car spotter. I can spot a car before I even see it. I can spot it just by the sound of its engine.

Mercedes-Benz! BMW! Ferrari!

Spotting a car has never been a problem for me. Grandfather taught me car spotting. Grandfather is the only other person in the entire village who can spot a car before he sees it.

"Grandfather, is it not true that you have been here your whole life spotting cars and

telling stories under the iroko tree?"
I ask.

Grandfather chuckles. "When
I was a young man there was no
excuse to sit under the iroko tree,"
he says. "I had many children. And
Grandmother kept my back bent
firmly over my carpentry work
in those days!"

"But what about all the
people wanting to hear
your stories?"
I ask him.

Grandfather knows all of
the stories of the Odu Ifa,
the history and wisdom
of our people. People
travel a long way to
hear Grandfather
recite those stories, and they pay him too.
It is said that if you listen well-well to the
Odu Ifa, you will hear the answer to all
your problems.

So what did people do when Grandfather
was a young man? Did they wait until he
had time to raise his head from his work?

"Very few people came to hear stories in
those days," Grandfather replies. "There was
no road."

No road? NO ROAD?

I stare at Grandfather. He chuckles again.

"Did you think there was always this
fine-fine road here?" Grandfather laughs.
"Not at all! Once upon a time, when the

geckos were as big as the mountains and the river ran with palm wine, this village could only be reached by trek-trek-trekking through the bush."

I cannot believe it!

"Is true!" Grandfather insists. "Before-before, if I wanted to reach the town, I had to creep past the hyenas and the cobras and the soldier ants."

My eyes grow even bigger.

"In those days there was little time and little opportunity for telling stories." Grandfather sighs. "Until one day I heard a small sound from far away. Every day it grew louder, until it was a commotion and a racket. I wanted to run through the bush—"

"Dodging the hyenas and the cobras and the soldier ants?" I interrupt.

"Dodging the hyenas and the cobras and the ants." Grandfather smiles. "But every time I looked up from my work, Grandmother shouted at me to continue. I knew how to dodge hyenas, cobras and ants, but I did not know how to dodge your grandmother!"

I cover my mouth to hide my smile. I do not know how to dodge Grandmother either!

"Then one day I could not bear it any longer," Grandfather continues.

"I sent your father off through the bush to investigate the commotion—"

"Dodging the hyenas and the cobras and the ants," I whisper.

"Dodging the hyenas and the cobras and the ants."

Grandfather nods. "It took him the whole day to go and to return, but the news he brought left even Grandmother's mouth empty."

"'A road!'" your father cried. "'A road is coming!'"

"And it was not long before a whole dusty commotion of men and machines arrived. They carved their way through the trees. They cut their way through the bush from one city to another. And when they left, they left the road behind them."

In our village we do not have electricity or even tap water. But thanks to the fact that we lie in the path of the road, we see Mercedes-Benz and BMW and Ferrari pass every single day! And so that was how the road had come to this electricity-forsaken village.

Na-wa-oh!

"Thanks to those mighty men and their mighty machines!" I shout.

Mama Coca-Cola arrives under the iroko tree. "But they have not come back, eh?" she grumbles. "Your mighty men and their mighty machines. They have not come back to repair the road! Just like a man to perform a mighty deed and then leave all the work to somebody else." Grandfather looks at me and raises his eyebrows. There is plenty that he could say about the faults of women, but he does not. It is not wise to insult somebody who cooks your food. That is what Grandfather has taught me.

And in fact Mama Coca-Cola is right. Those mighty men and their mighty machines have never come back. There are holes in the road now. Big-big holes.

And every rainy season those holes get
bigger and bigger and bigger. This year one
of those holes became so big it swallowed
a Lamborghini. Another hole swallowed an
entire bus! This rainy season the floods and
the mud are so bad the owners cannot even
tow their broken vehicles away.

So now any car that comes along the road
from one direction sees that Lamborghini
crumpled up like a crisp packet in a muddy
hole. Each and every car and bus and taxi
quickly turns around and goes back the way
it came. And any vehicle that comes from

the other direction reverses fast when it sees
the top of the bus that was swallowed up
by the hole.

So now there are no cars for me to spot!
No cars at-all, at-all. And how can I be the
No. 1 car spotter if there are no cars to spot?
What am I supposed to do?

And Mama Coca-Cola is annoyed
because now all her customers are driving
another way and buying some other chop
madam's food instead.

Grandmother and Mama and my sister,
Sissy, arrive under the iroko tree.

"When will this rain ever stop?"
Mama asks.

Grandmother shakes
her fist at the sky.
"Already it has rained
for one month more
than it normally
rains," she complains.

"And the crops in the fields are beginning to rot," Mama says in a worried voice. "We will be hungry next year if this rain does not stop."

"Last time this happened, did our village starve?" Sissy asks, scared.

"This has never happened before," Grandmother says. "Not in my time or my mother's time or my grandmother's time or my great-grandmother's time."

"How do you know, Grandmother?" Sissy asks.

"If it had happened before, there would be a story about it," Grandmother replies. "We would all know."

It is true. We know about the time there was a great fire. And the time hippopotamus came from the river into the village. And the time soldiers came and took men from the village away. We know many-many things that happened long before any of us were born. But we have never heard about the rainy season continuing into the dry season.

"This rain means trouble," says Grandmother. "Waiting for this rain to stop is like waiting for a baby that refuses to be born. With a baby I would know what to do. But with the rain, what are we supposed to do? When a person goes wrong, that is only to be expected. People need to be corrected from time to time. But when the rain goes wrong, who can correct the rain?"

Grandmother looks angry. Mama looks worried.

"Our crops..." she whispers.

Suddenly I hear a sound I know.

"Hummer! Hummer!" I shout.

The Hummer belongs to Mr Johnson, the American engineer who is working on the new bridge on the other side of town. He passes here from time to time. He is the only one on the road with a vehicle big enough to tackle the holes!

We all run down to the chop-house to greet him. Mama Coca-Cola is quick to light her cooking fires and heat her frying pans. This particular American can eat enough akara to feed a busload of people.

Mr Johnson runs from his SUV into the chop-house. By the time he comes through the door, his shirt is as wet as if he had been

building his bridge single-handedly. "It sure can rain in this place," he says.

"It is not supposed to be raining," Grandmother says. "It should have stopped by now."

"According to who?" The American laughs. "Never trust a weather forecaster!"

"According to me!" Grandmother says firmly.

Mr Johnson is wise enough to stop laughing.

"It has never rained this long before," I say quickly. "Never before in history."

"Oh!" Mr Johnson smiles. "When does it normally stop?"

"One month ago," Grandfather says quietly.

Now it is Mr Johnson's turn to look serious. "It is climate change," he says. "In some places there is too much sun, others too much rain or wind."

We all look at one another and frown.

"This is happening everywhere?" Grandmother asks.

"All over the world." Mr Johnson sighs.

"But why?" asks Mama. "Why is this happening?"

"It is because of us." The American shrugs. "Our big cars and aeroplanes and electric power plants. We have poisoned the sky."

Grandmother cries out.

We look at one another again. We have poisoned the sky? But we are not the ones with cars or aeroplanes or power plants. Why are we being punished too?

Suddenly Mama Coca-Cola stands up and straightens her headtie. "The road must be repaired so that the cars can pass, rain or no rain," she says. "Climatic change or no climatic whatever – I need customers."

Mama Coca-Cola puts akara in front of Mr Johnson. Then she opens the door. Everybody looks at her in surprise.

"Where are you going?" Grandfather asks.

"To see the government." Mama Coca-Cola steps out into the rain.

I dodge out and follow her.

Mama Coca-Cola is a big woman. She walks through the rain and the floods like a ship ploughing through the sea. I follow her, skinny and quick as a lizard. By the time we reach town, Mama Coca-Cola is panting.

"Where is a taxi when a person needs one?" she grumbles.

The only taxis are rusting in the mud.

I follow Mama Coca-Cola to the local government offices. It is said that if you annoy the government officials, they will make sure that your family does not prosper. They will tell you that you need a business permit. Then you will find that you cannot get it because it does not exist! Who wants to risk that?

Mama Coca-Cola is determined, but I can see she is afraid. She stands in the waiting room with her face clenched, but her hands are shaking. When her name is called she grabs my hand.

In the inner room, two men are bent over desks piled high with papers.

"Yes," says one of them. He does not even look up.

Mama Coca-Cola clutches my hand even tighter.

"The road is broken…" her voice squeaks.

The official looks up. "The road? The road?" he says sternly.

"It needs repairing…" Mama Coca-Cola squeaks again.

"Repair de road? Repair de road?" the official shouts. "Who do you people think you are? An order like that must come from federal government. Not from a fat, illiterate chop-madam like you who cannot even read and write!"

Mama Coca-Cola's head droops. She says nothing more. How can someone who cannot read win against someone who can? They can read all the laws and decipher all the papers. They can curse you with a court order or the withdrawal of a business licence.

"Next!" shouts the official.

Slowly, Mama Coca-Cola walks
all the way back to the village,
her head bent. Slowly, I follow.
In the chop-house,
everybody is
waiting. Mama
Coca-Cola
cannot speak.

"They insulted
her," I whisper.

We all
stand silent.
Grandmother has
her hand on Mama Coca-Cola's
shoulder. The rain is loud on the roof.

I look out at the road. It has holes that are
badder than a Lamborghini. Holes that even
our bad-boy taxi drivers are afraid of.

Until the road is repaired, no car will pass
here. And I will no longer be the No. 1 car
spotter. I will be just a village boy.

I whisper this to Grandfather. Grandfather looks at me.

"The reason you are a No. 1 car spotter is because you have a No. 1 brain. Use your brain to fix the road."

I look back at Grandfather.

I am only a village boy without a single naira to my name. And to fix this road will take more money than all the cars that I have ever spotted are worth. Grandfather knows that. But if he thinks that I can do it, then I must try.

Lucky Shorts

It may be true that I have a No. 1 brain,
but I still have not found a solution for the
broken road. The holes are now the size of
craters on the moon. All the cars go another
way from one city to another.

This is bad. Very bad. What use is a car
spotter without cars to spot? It is enough
to make even a tough boy like me cry.

Mama Coca-Cola has been
crying because her chop-house
is empty. Her customers are
eating the akara of other
chop madams in other
villages. She can no
longer afford to send her
son, Coca-Cola, to school.

Mama has been crying because now
there are no taxi drivers and there is no
news of my father.

Even Grandfather has been
fighting back tears. He sits
alone day after day under the
iroko tree, with nobody to
listen to all his stories.

But tomorrow is the
wedding of my cousin
Homework, and preparing for a wedding
can dry any amount of tears.

So for now Mama Coca-Cola is happy.

She is doing what she does best: cooking mountains of delicious akara for the wedding guests.

Mama is happy. She is finishing sewing our wedding clothes with Grandmother. All the bride's family will be wearing clothes from this same red cloth. But Mama and Grandmother plan for our outfits to be the finest of all.

And Grandfather is happy. He is thinking of all the new stories he will hear at the wedding, stories contained in other old men's heads.

Now it is only me who is not happy. I am watching the holes in the road grow bigger, wishing some vehicle would pass. Even an old Bedford bus with its doors hanging off would make me shout now!

"No. 1!" Grandmother looks up from her sewing. "First thing tomorrow you must run down the road to call a taxi!"

I look at Grandmother, confused. "Taxi?" I ask.

Grandmother rolls her eyes. "Yes!" she shouts. "Tomorrow you must call a taxi! Is that so hard to understand? You spend so much time spotting cars that your brains have leaked out of your ears!"

I look at Grandmother and frown. That is not true. It is when she pulls my ears that my brains leak out!

"At times there are more important things than car spotting," Grandfather says, joining in with Grandmother.

I look at Grandfather reproachfully. How can he say such a thing? And they are wrong! There is nothing, nothing in the world, more important than car spotting.

And I can prove it right now! I draw myself up tall and speak loudly.

"As the No. 1 car spotter, I can officially tell you now that there are no cars on this road. There are no taxis to call. Not today and not tomorrow!"

For a moment nobody moves. They have been so busy thinking about the wedding that they had forgotten that the road is broken.

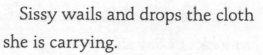

Sissy wails and drops the cloth she is carrying.

Mama's mouth falls open and pins spill all over the floor.

Grandmother flings her arms up into the air and knocks Grandfather's cap off his head.

But I am not worried. I have a No. 1 solution already! "Shall I prepare the Cow-rolla?" I ask.

"Everybody will stare at us!" Sissy cries.

"And our clothes will be ruined by the mud!" Grandmother shouts.

"And people will laugh!" Mama wails.

I look at Grandfather.

"Prepare the Cow-rolla." Grandfather sighs.

Mama and Grandmother and Sissy cannot stop crying. Every time one of them stops, another one starts. But not me. I don't care how we get to the wedding as long as we go.

My stomach rumbles in anticipation. The best thing about weddings is the food. Every mama and grandmother cooks whatever she cooks best. There are sure to be towers of fried plantains, mountains of creamy pounded yams and buckets of the most delicious stews that you could dream of.

Early the next morning I run to hitch the cows to the Cow-rolla. I quickly wash myself outside with a bucket of water. Then I run back into the house to dress.

Mama is
ready, in a big
red head-tie
and bubba
blouse and
wrappa skirt.
Grandmother's
head-tie
is bigger.
Sissy's dress
could even be
considered pretty – but not by me!

I put on my smart new red shirt. Then
my mother pulls her bottom-box from
underneath her bed. Inside it are stored
all of our best clothes, the ones saved for
special occasions. My mother takes out my
smart trouser.

I take the trouser. I try to put it on. My
legs enter and the trouser reaches over my
bom-bom. But it refuses to close at the front.

"Mama...?" I say.

Mama looks at me. "Oh no!" Mama covers her mouth.

Sissy looks at me. "Hee-hee!" Sissy laughs.

Grandmother looks at me. She reaches forward and pulls both sides of the trouser towards each other. But no matter how hard Grandmother pulls, the trouser will not close!

Grandfather comes into the room. "Hurry! Hurry!" he complains.

"He cannot go like this!" Grandmother points at me.

"And there is no time to adjust the trouser." Mama closes her eyes.

"So pin it!" Grandfather says crossly.

"What pin will reach across that gap?" Grandmother snorts.

"He will disgrace us," Sissy wails.

"He will not!" says Grandmother firmly.
"He will stay here."

"No!" I shout. "No! No!"

"Just let the boy wear another trouser,"
Grandfather says.

Grandmother and Mama turn on him.

"What trouser does he have without
holes? Without tears? Without stains?
You want him to go to the wedding wearing
rags?"

"All right! All right!" Grandfather raises
his hands.

Grandmother looks at me.

"This is what happens when you sit
around eating akara and drinking Coca-
Cola with American boys instead of helping
your Grandmother to collect firewood.
Now you are too fat for your own
clothes," she says.

"Coca-Cola's grandmother will
look after you, No. 1," Mama says.

I watch my family climb into the Cow-
rolla without me. I watch my best friend,
Coca-Cola, and Mama Coca-Cola and Uncle
Go-Easy and my cousins, Tuesday and
Emergency, and Nike and Aunty Fine-Fine
climb in with them.

I watch them all go without me. I cry
loudly and I don't care who in the village
hears me. I cry for so long that soon my
shirt becomes wet.

Then I hear a familiar sound. I look over the compound wall. It is Mr Johnson's Hummer. No mud is too deep for its gigantic wheels.

The Hummer stops in front of the chop-house. Mr Johnson gets out. He looks at the closed, empty chop-house. He looks up at the village.

"No. 1?" Mr Johnson shouts. "Where is everybody?"

I rub the tear marks from my face. Mr Johnson is walking up to our compound.

He is going to see me standing here with an open trouser!

I suck in my breath! I squeeze in my stomach! I fasten my trouser! I cannot breathe!

"Where is Mama Coca-Cola? Where is everybody?" Mr Johnson asks.

"They have gone to a wedding." My voice squeaks like a rat in a corn bin.

The small-small trouser is making it impossible for air to enter my body.

"But I have come all this way to eat Mama Coca-Cola's akara," Mr Johnson complains.

I look at the big, hungry American. I look at his big, gas-guzzling car. Suddenly I have a No. 1 idea!

"Mama Coca-Cola and her fine-fine akara have gone ahead to the wedding," I squeak. "At the wedding there are mountains of akara. And buckets of palm wine to wash it all down."

Mr Johnson groans with hunger.

"And I am waiting to escort you there!" I announce.

"Me?" Mr Johnson looks puzzled.

"Of course," I squeak. "It is always an honour to have an American at a wedding."

Mr Johnson smiles.

"We'd better hurry up," I squeak quickly. "Or we will miss the food."

"Let's go, then!" Mr Johnson hurries back to his car.

I follow slowly with my legs very straight, otherwise my trousers will break. Mr Johnson looks at me and frowns.

"Traditional African wedding trouser," I squeak once more.

I manoeuvre myself with straight-straight legs carefully into the cool, air-conditioned Hummer. I cannot believe my luck. No more crying loudly for me! I will arrive at the wedding in more style than the bride herself.

It is a very slow journey. It is necessary to navigate craters the size of schools and mud as deep as a hippopotamus' bath. By the time we arrive, the wedding party is already well under way. Everybody is eating and dancing and shouting happily.

"Let's go eat!" I squeak over the sound of high-life ju-ju music.

I spot Grandfather sitting with the other old men, nodding his head to somebody else's story. I see Grandmother standing with the other old women, talking loud and proud. I see Sissy laughing behind her hand with the other girls.

I do not want them to see me. So I avoid them all. I want no wahalla, no palava, no trouble at-all, at-all.

Then, just as I am filling my plate for the

third time with fried chicken and pounded
yam and goat stew, Sissy spots me.

"How did you get here?" she hisses.

My mouth is crammed with fried chicken.
Of course I am too polite to talk with my
mouth full of food. So I ignore her.

"If you continue to eat like a dog, your
trouser will burst." Sissy eyes my trousers.

I turn my back on Sissy. But I stop eating.
Then the drums begin. If you have never
heard wedding drums, you do not know
what it is to dance.

My feet begin to tap. My knees begin to bend. My bom-bom begins to wiggle. And suddenly I jump onto the dance floor!

I see Sissy and Mama watching me, their eyes popping like frogs' eyes. I see Mama with her hands over her face. I see Grandmother with her hands on her hips. Don't mind them! I am enjoying myself. I shake, I wiggle, then – just as I leap into the air – CRACK!

My trouser splits right up the back. And there I am in the middle of the dance floor with my bom-bom sticking out.

Everybody is silent. Then they shriek and laugh and point at me. I am frozen. Faster than a snake, Grandmother is on the dance floor. Her strong fingers clamp around my ear. She drags me away.

Grandmother pushes me into the back of the Hummer. Some small children are outside, still laughing and pointing at me. I look away. I do not want them to see me crying.

On the floor of the Hummer are empty packets of sweets. And one old football boot. It belongs to LeRoy, Mr Johnson's son. There is something else as well. Something red. I pick up a pair of red football shorts!

LeRoy always used to bring his football shorts to the village for when we played football together. He used to say they were his lucky shorts. Now they are my lucky shorts too!

Quick as a World Cup changeover I jump out of my broken trouser and into those shorts. I leap out of the Hummer and back onto the dance floor!

Once again I am jumping and twisting and shaking. Once again everybody is staring at me. But this time nobody is laughing. This time everybody is clapping and whistling.

I am the No. 1 car spotter. No. 1 at spotting cars and No. 1 at spotting shorts too! That's why I am the coolest, hottest, baddest and most definitely the No. 1 boy at this wedding!

The No. 1 Goat

I am the No. 1 car spotter. The No. 1 car spotter in my village.

But now there are no cars except for the Hummer. What use is a No. 1 car spotter without any cars?

And what use is a No. 1 roadside chop-house restaurant without any customers?

Every day Mama Coca-Cola sits alone outside her empty chop-house with her head in her hands. Today she calls Coca-Cola and me.

"Take the brown goat with the crooked horn," she says. "Take 'am for market and sell 'am."

I look at Coca-Cola. This means things are very, very bad.

Grandmother shakes her head when I tell her where I am going.

"When people start selling their goats things only get worse," she says. "And that goat market is a bad place. It is full of thieves. It is no place for foolish boys."

The goat market is far. It is not the market where we go to sell our tomatoes and our palm oil. It is not in the town where we go to complain to the authorities about the road.

Mama sighs. "Oh, Ma," she says. "Coca-Cola should not go alone."

So I help Coca-Cola chase the brown goat away from the rest of the herd and into the bush. We walk through the bush. The mud

sticks to our
legs. The goat
bleats nervously.
She is missing her
herd. Coca-Cola and I are
nervous too. It is far to the goat market.
And we have never gone alone before.

Suddenly I hear other goats bleating and
boys shouting. Then I see boys herding
many goats through the bush. The boys
stare at us and look at one another.

Suddenly one boy runs towards us. He
throws one stone and then another. The
stones land between us and Mama Coca-
Cola's goat. The goat runs. She runs into the
other boys' goat herd. I cannot believe it!

"Das our goat!" I shout. "Leave her alone!"
The boys laugh.

"Das our goat now!" one of them shouts
back.

The boys walk away, herding the goats
in front of them.

Coca-Cola and I look at each other. Those boys have stolen our goat. Just like that!

I chase after the boys, shouting. Two of them turn back. They push me down into the mud. One of them kicks me.

"Dat goat belongs to us now!" he shouts.

Then they run away. I get up to chase them. Coca-Cola grabs my arm. "Dey will beat you again!" Coca-Cola is crying.

I follow Coca-Cola back towards the village. His shoulders are shaking. What will he say to his mother? Now they are even poorer than before!

I stop and look back. The other boys are already far in the distance. I let Coca-Cola walk on. I turn back and run after the goat boys. I stay well back. I do not let them see me.

I follow the boys all the way to the goat market. It is near a big town. The town is on a small hill with a thick wall all around it. I can see the rounded shapes of places where people like to pray.

The goat market is outside the town.
It is thick with the smell of goats and loud
with bleating and the shouting of men.
It is bigger than our entire village.

I lose sight of the boys. But it does not
matter. I push through the people
until I see what I am looking for.

Iroko trees casting their shade
and old men sitting beneath
them.

I go and prostrate myself
to the old men. I do not say
anything until one of them asks,
"Wha' is it?"

"A poor widow sent a goat
here to be sold. Instead it has
been stolen," I say. "A brown one.
With a crooked horn."

The old men murmur. "Who
was witness to this crime?" one
of them asks.

"I was witness," I say. "And my friend, the widow's son. We were bringing the goat here together when some other boys overtook us and stole the goat."

"Where is the widow's son now?" the old men ask.

"He returned to our village when the boys beat me."

The old men's murmurs grow loud. "They beat you, you say?" one of them asks.

"They pushed me to the ground and kicked me," I say.

"Without a witness how will you prove

that what you say is true?" the old men ask.

"I will run and get my friend!" I answer. "We will show you the goat. She has a crooked horn."

"You boys will say it is your goat and the other boys will say it is theirs. And how will we know the truth?"

The old men turn from me and begin to talk of other matters.

My belly is full of anger. My heart is full of shame. My eyes are full of tears. I push my way back through the many people and their many-many goats. Soon I am near the edge of the market.

"... a crooked horn!" I hear a man shouting. "Since when did one of my goats have a crooked horn? And where is the big black goat with the white shoulder?"

I look towards the shouting man. Grandmother was right. This goat market is a bad-bad place.

The man who is shouting is a big man. He wears a long embroidered robe and a blue cloth wound around his head. Beads hang around his neck. A stick trembles in his hand as he shouts. And cowering in front of him are the boys who stole Mama Coca-Cola's goat!

It is her crooked horned goat that the big man is shouting about! It is her goat that the big man knows has been stolen!

I do not waste one second. I run straight back to the iroko trees. When I arrive in front of the old men I do not even wait to prostrate myself.

"I have found a witness!" I shout. "A good witness. Come! Please come!"

The old men look at me. Sweat is running down my face. My belly is heaving. Slowly one old man gets up. And then another. And another. Slowly they follow me.

My heart is hammering inside my chest.

Please don't let that shouting man be gone before we reach them.

Yes! The man is still there shouting. And the boys are still there cowering. And the herd of goats is still milling about with Mama Coca-Cola's small brown goat.

"So you have lost my goat! My big black goat! And you think you can replace it with this small crooked horn?"

There are many people watching.
The elders listen.

"You say there is a goat here that does not belong to you?" one of them suddenly asks. "Which one?"

The big man mumbles angrily. He had not noticed the elders listening. But he points out Mama Coca-Cola's small brown goat with the crooked horn.

The elders look at one another. "This boy told us that a brown goat with a crooked horn was stolen from him," one of them says.

Mama Coca-Cola's goat is standing on the edge of the herd. She does not know the other goats. It is easy to go and stand beside her and put my hand on her neck.

She knows me. Everybody can see that.

"And how did this goat come to be in your herd?" the elders asks the man.

"That's just what I am asking these useless boys," the man says angrily. "They are supposed to herd my goats, not lose some and add others!"

He waves his stick again. The boys cower. They are silent.

"They stole her from me in the bush!" I shout angrily. "They pushed me in the dirt and kicked me."

I raise my shirt to show the marks. All around us people murmur angrily. The boys cower lower. The man's eyes bulge.

The elder raises his stick.

"This goat is now returned to this boy," he says. "He will choose another goat to right the wrong. And he will choose yet another to soothe his bruises."

The people murmur in agreement and nod their heads. The big man shouts even louder.

"It was these useless boys who stole that boy's goat and kicked him! Not me! Why do you repay him with my goats?"

The elders answer quietly. "You chose these boys to herd your goats and you are responsible for their actions. They have nothing to repay this boy with. But you have a lot."

Again people murmur in agreement. The big man's shoulders sag.

"Pick your goats," he says to me.

Two goats! Two new goats for Mama Coca-Cola! I look carefully at the herd. Grandmother is always telling me which goats are best.

Not the big ones, she says. *The fat ones. With strong legs. And small horns.*

Carefully I choose my goats. A white goat and a brown goat. They are not the

biggest in the herd. But they are the fattest.
With strong legs to carry them to the
sweetest grass in the bush and small horns
that do not weigh
them down or
lead them into
fights.

The elders nod their approval. The people
smile. The big man scowls.

I herd the three goats away. I sell Mama
Coca-Cola's goat. I herd the other two back
into the bush. It is for Mama Coca-Cola
to decide what she wants to do with these
fine goats.

When I am not far from the village I see a small figure running towards me.

"Coca-Cola!" I shout.

Coca-Cola runs even faster. He throws his arms around my neck.

"I am so happy to see you!" Coca-Cola cries. "I thought you had followed those boys. I was afraid..."

I grin and put my arms around Coca-Cola's neck. I tell him the whole story.

"Na-wa-oh!" Coca-Cola looks at me with admiration in his eyes.

When we reach the village I tell the story again, this time to Mama Coca-Cola. I give her the goat money and the two new goats.

"Na-wa-oh!" Mama Coca-Cola shrieks so loudly that the whole village comes running.

I tell the story once again. I will never tire of this story!

"You truly are the No. 1." Mama shakes her head, smiling.

"Pick one goat, No. 1," Mama Coca-Cola says. "Pick one for your bruises."

"For true?" I stare at Mama Coca-Cola.

"You have earned it, No. 1," she nods.

And the whole village cheers.

I pick the No. 1 goat. I smile my No. 1 smile. I am the No. 1. The No. 1 car spotter in my village. And now I am the proud owner of one fine goat. My goat is so fat, she is so fine and she belongs to me. That must make her the No. 1 goat in the village herd!

Government Goes to Town

I am the No. 1 car spotter. The No. 1 car spotter in my village.

It used to be that our village was a happy village because of the No. 1 road that carried cars through it.

Mama Coca-Cola was happy because the road brought her many-many No. 1 customers to buy her akara and soft drinks.

Coca-Cola was happy because his mother, Mama Coca-Cola, made enough money to send him to school. And this meant that one day he would be a big man in the big city.

Uncle Go-Easy was happy because when he had finished fishing in the river, he could sell his fish to Mama Coca-Cola's rich customers and then sit and drink Fanta with the taxi drivers.

Mama was happy because passing taxi drivers brought news of my father, whose business is in a taxi park in the city.

My cousins were happy because the city people driving by gave them an idea of what

was cool and what was not.

"Look a' dat!" Emergency would shout, pointing at a man in a Porsche wearing his baseball hat backwards.

Grandfather was happy because cars and buses and taxis brought people who had come for the sole purpose of listening to him recite the Odu Ifa.

And I, I am the No. 1 car spotter. I was happy just to spot cars. The one and only Firebird

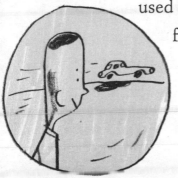

used to pass here on its way from one city to another. And the professor who drove it used to stop and call me his friend.

But now there are no cars to spot. There are no customers for the chop-house and there is no money for school. There is no news of my father and there are no clues as to what is cool. There are no listeners and no friends.

We are all unhappy. We sit in the chop-house every day, sheltering from the rain and wondering what to do.

Today it is Grandfather who gets up from his seat. He draws himself up tall.

"What are you doing?" Grandmother asks.

"I am the elder," Grandfather says, his voice as stiff as his back. "I must go and talk to these government official people. I must make them see sense."

"No!" Mama cries. "They will insult you too!"

"They will curse our family!" Grandmother wails. "That is what they do to people who challenge them."

"It is my duty," Grandfather replies. "No. 1, take me there."

I hitch up the Cow-rolla, and Coca-Cola and I take Grandfather into town, all the way to the government offices.

I do not want to go back to that place. What would those men do to a boy who disturbed them twice?

This is what I am wondering as we wait in the hot and dusty waiting room. The white is falling off the walls. The calendar is from last year.

At last it is our turn.

"What can I do for you?" The official is still looking at his papers.

"Good morning," Grandfather replies politely. "I hope that you and your family are well."

The official does not answer.

"I trust that your mother is well?" Grandfather asks. "And your wife?"

"Do you want to tell me your problem or do you want to waste my time?" The official sucks his teeth.

Grandfather draws in his breath. It pains him to communicate in an impolite and undignified fashion.

"The road that passes my village is broken. Cars are not using it any more. Our businesses are suffering."

"So?" the official asks.

Grandfather draws in another deep breath. Grandfather hates rudeness.

"The road needs to be fixed," Grandfather says. "I understand that you have money from the federal government to deal with such emergencies."

"And who are you?" Now the official looks up from his papers.

"Who are you to decide what is an emergency and what is not?"

"I am an elder," Grandfather says at last.

"You are nothing but an old man."

The official sucks his teeth again.

He calls through to the waiting room.

"Next!"

Grandfather looks at the official. The official looks at his papers.

"Remember me to your mother," Grandfather says. "Tell her Baba Femi hopes her health is improved."

The official's jaw drops.

Grandfather does not wait for it to close.

We walk slowly back through the town. People greet Grandfather as we pass. He does not reply. At last somebody asks, "Baba, what happen?"

Grandfather tells them the whole story. People shake their heads and suck their teeth.

"Those so-called officials are bad," one says. "They drain government money straight into their own pockets. Their children go to fancy schools overseas. Their wives drive fancy cars."

"Maybe it is their salary that pays for all that," another argues.

"Anybody who works for the government and can afford to send their children to expensive schools is a thief whether their salary pays for it or not."

Somebody else agrees. "That money is government money and it should be going to help poor people to better themselves!"

The people shake their heads again. Grandfather sighs. Somebody pats him on the arm.

"You tried, Baba. You tried."

"You would have to be friends with the chief of police himself to get this road fixed," somebody jokes as we walk away.

I immediately stop walking. For one second I stare straight ahead of me. A light bulb has come on inside my brain. I know what to do to fix the road. But how?

As if by magic, I hear the Hummer. And here is Mr Johnson at the wheel.

I wave and shout and the Hummer stops.

"Wha's up, No. 1?" Mr Johnson asks.

"We need to go to the city," I say.

Grandfather looks at me. Grandfather has never been to the city before. And he prefers to spot cars from the safety of the iroko tree rather than drive about as if he were inside a computer game. But he nods.

"Take us there," Grandfather says to Mr Johnson. And he climbs right into the Hummer.

Mr Johnson looks surprised.

Sometimes Grandfather forgets that he is only the chief of our village and not of the whole world.

"It is an emergency," I say, following Grandfather into the Hummer.

"OK." Mr Johnson shrugs.

Mr Johnson is a good man.

We pass Coca-Cola waiting with the Cow-rolla. I open the window.

Grandfather shouts, "Return to the village! We go come!"

All the way to the city, Grandfather clings onto his seat as if he might fall from the car. But when we arrive, he forgets all about the fact that he is sitting in a moving vehicle. His neck twists like a lizard as he stares at the skyscrapers and hotels and neon lights.

When a Rolls-Royce passes us on the road, Grandfather whistles.

"Where to, boss?" Mr Johnson asks.

Grandfather looks at me.

"Take us to the police station," I say. "We need to see a friend."

And Grandfather laughs.

Mr Johnson raises his eyebrows, but he does not ask any questions. He drops us at the police station and waves goodbye.

I lead Grandfather up the tall steps to the main door. I have been here before.

"Yes?" There is a policewoman sitting behind a desk.

"We have come to see the Chief of Police," I say.

The policewoman looks at me.
Then she looks at Grandfather.
She looks us up and down.

"Have you got an
appointment?" she asks.

"No," I say.

"Then you cannot see
him," the policewoman
says.

"Please. Just tell him—"

"No," says the policewoman firmly.

A telephone starts to ring.

"We have come a long way." Grandfather's
voice is low.

"You are wasting my time," the
policewoman replies.

She turns away to answer the telephone.

"No. 1!" a voice shouts behind us. "No. 1!
Is that you?"

All the policemen in the building jump to
attention. The policewoman in front of us

drops the phone. I turn around. Running up the steps into the building is the Chief of Police himself!

I smile my No. 1 smile!

The Chief of Police grabs my hand and shakes it. He shakes Grandfather's hand.

"Cancel all my appointments!" he says to the policewoman. "This is the No. 1 car spotter. The boy who helped me to capture that gang of international car thieves."

"I hope you told her who you were?" the chief asks us.

Grandfather looks at the policewoman.
The policewoman trembles.
"We were just getting to that."
Grandfather smiles.

The Chief of Police takes us to my
favourite chop-house, Pizza Hut. While we
are eating pizza I tell him the whole story.
About how the road was built years and
years and years ago. But how it had never
been fixed. And how after years and years

and years of rain it was now broken and no cars could pass any more.

The Chief of Police frowns. "Have you informed the authorities?" he asks.

"We have," says Grandfather.

"And what do they say?"

Grandfather is silent. Then he says, "They said it was not for us to decide what to do with government money."

The Chief of Police sucks his teeth. "Useless people," he says. He snatches up his phone. "Get me my SUV!"

And so Grandfather and I travel back to the town in the SUV of the Chief of Police himself. With a full police escort.

We pull up outside the offices of the town authorities with all the sirens blaring. The two officials come running out of the door. They begin to salute the Chief of Police. Then they remember that they are not policemen. They begin to prostrate themselves. Then they remember that they are officials. They begin to shake his hand. Then they remember that they are only lowly officials.

"Who is in charge here?" the Chief of Police barks.

"I am, sa!" says the official who had spoken to us.

"Then you are responsible, personally responsible, for the fact that the road from the city to the village of my good friend is in such a terrible state!"

The official looks at Grandfather and me. His eyes widen as he recognizes us.

"We were unaware of the true extent of the damage," he says.

Grandfather clears his throat.

"This gentleman did come to our offices," the official admits.

"And?" asks the Chief of Police.

"And we did not believe that he was qualified to assess road conditions." The official looks at the ground.

"So did you drive down the road to assess the conditions yourselves?" the Chief of Police asks.

Now the official looks like a fish on a hook, wriggling and gasping and unable to escape.

"Let me see you assess the damage now." The chief motions to the officials to jump into their own cars. The two officials climb slowly into two brand new, shiny BMWs.

The whole
convoy sets off,
with the BMWs
leading the way.

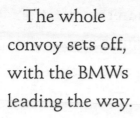

As soon as the road turns in the direction of the village, the holes as big as moon craters appear. The BMWs slow down. Then stop. Any idiot can see that no car can cross even the first crater.

Suddenly one of the BMWs revs its engine and shoots forward. Grandfather starts to chuckle.

The BMW shoots into the crater and its wheels are immediately engulfed in deep, thick mud.

"Bravo!" Grandfather claps his hands.

The second BMW tries to creep slowly around the edge of the crater, keeping two of its wheels on the road. But slowly it slides down and comes to rest on the bus that had failed at the same manoeuvre weeks ago.

"Bravo!"
Grandfather claps
again.

After a
while the two
officials creep
out of the hole.
They are covered from head to foot in mud.

The Chief of Police winds his window
down.

"What is your official assessment of the
road?" he asks.

"It is impassable, sir." The officials hang
their head.

"Is that so?" asks the chief.

"Yes, sir."

"And what do you intend to do about it?" the Chief of Police asks.

"We must repair it, sir," the officials reply.

"And make sure you do!" roars the Chief of Police. "Because now I have my eye on you! And I will not take it off. Not ever!"

The Chief
of Police
drives us back
to the village.
Mama and
Grandmother
and Mama
Coca-Cola immediately set to cooking a
feast of fried chicken and jolloff rice. The
chief eats as if he has never eaten before.
But Grandfather does not eat anything.

"That pizza-pizza was too much for an
old man's stomach," he groans.

We all laugh.

Soon there will be customers buying Mama Coca-Cola's akara and Uncle Go-Easy's fish. Soon Coca-Cola will be back at school and Emergency and Tuesday will know what's cool. Soon Mama will have news of Papa, and Grandfather will have people to tell stories to. Soon the entire village will be happy. And all because of me. Even though I am a village boy without a single naira in his pocket, I have found the solution to our broken road. Because I am the No. 1 car spotter. The No. 1 car spotter in the world!

Atinuke was born in Nigeria
and grew up in both Africa and the UK.
She works as a traditional oral storyteller
in schools and theatres all over the world.
All of Atinuke's many children's books
are set in the Africa of her childhood.
Atinuke lives on a mountain overlooking
the sea in West Wales with her two sons.

Warwick Johnson Cadwell
lives by the Sussex seaside with his
smashing family and pets. Most of
his time is spent drawing, or thinking
about drawing, but for a change of
scenery he also skippers boats.
The No. 1 Car Spotter and the Broken Road
is his seventh book for Walker Books.